This book is presented to:

Renee

On the occasion of:

her 22nd year
celebration

From:

The Pittmans!

Honor him, for he is your lord.
Psalm 45:11

A Warrior Prince for God ™

By Kelly Chapman
Illustrated by Jeff Ebbeler

HARVEST HOUSE PUBLISHERS

EUGENE, OREGON

may this be one of many in your library for your ministry

Follow His will bravely!

To the real Warrior Princes
in my life—Luke, Brit, Dad, and all boys
who desire to be brave and noble warriors for Jesus.

A Warrior Prince for God™

Text Copyright © 2010 by Kelly Chapman
Artwork Copyright © 2010 by Jeff Ebbeler

Published by Harvest House Publishers
Eugene, Oregon 97402
www.harvesthousepublishers.com

ISBN 978-0-7369-2895-3

Design and production by Mary pat Design, Westport, Connecticut

Printed in China

10 11 12 13 14 15 16 / LP / 10 9 8 7 6 5 4 3 2 1

What is Warrior Prince Academy?
For more information, please visit www.royalpurpose.com

Chapter One – The Big Game

Once upon a real time, there lived a boy named Luke. He dreamed of becoming a courageous warrior who was noble and brave, but there was a problem. Luke was afraid. His fear kept him from believing he could ever be a real warrior. Or could he?

"It's the bottom of the ninth inning. The Warriors are down one run with two outs, bases are loaded, and Luke Allen is up to bat. This is the most important play of the game!" the announcer reported.

"Go, Luke! You can do it!" cheered Luke's mom and dad.

"Ruff! Ruff!" chimed his dog, Burpie.

"Wait for the pitch Luke!" reminded Coach Britmore.

"Don't strike out like last time *or else!*" threatened Double from third base. Agreeing with his twin brother, Trouble shouted, "Yeah!" from second base and kept a menacing watch on Luke. They were inseparable. Wherever Double was, Trouble followed.

With so many voices, Luke found it hard to focus and be brave.

"Here comes the pitch," the announcer said. "It's a swing and a *miss!*"

"Steee-rike *one!*" shouted the umpire.

"Steee-rike *two!*"

"Stee-rike *three!* Game over!"

Luke dropped his head and dragged his bat to the dugout, found a seat, and put his head in his hands.

"Don't worry about it," Harris said. "Technically the ball traveled faster than the average kid our size could hit." Harris was the smartest kid at school. He had a formula and an answer for everything.

"Try telling that to Double and Trouble," said Luke under his breath.

"You played a tough game," said Coach Britmore. "I'm proud of you. We lost, but you can hold your heads high. After all, we're not just a baseball team called *The Warriors*, we are God's warriors! Remember when we talked about King David and his mighty men? They stood side by side even in tough times. I expect you to do the same. We're all for one and one for all!"

With that proclamation, the entire team cheered!

But Luke couldn't focus on anything Coach Britmore said. He was too busy dreading what Double and Trouble might do to him.

"Cheer up, Luke," encouraged Harris, as they walked from the dugout. "By my calculations, the percentage of people who'll remember your last at bat is practically next to nothing. Besides, the campout's tonight!"

"As long as the twins don't find out," said Tomás, Luke's other best friend.

"Shhh! They might hear you," warned Harris.

"Campout? We love campouts! Right, Trouble?" asked Double.

"Right—especially when we're not invited," snickered Trouble.

"Uh, my tent only sleeps three, and uh..." Luke stammered, trying to explain.

"Luke, time to go!" Lukes's dad called to the boys.

Relieved, Luke quickly said, "Sorry—gotta go!" as he, Tomás, and Harris ran toward the car.

"Wow, that was a close one!" gasped Tomás. "You don't think they'll show up, do you?"

"Nah," said Luke. "Besides, Burpie's our watch dog!"

By the time they got home, Luke was so excited about setting up for the campout that he forgot all about Double and Trouble.

The boys unrolled their sleeping bags, ate pizza, and shared spooky stories. Before long, it was time to turn off their flashlights and go to sleep.

"Psst! Luke, do you think Double and Trouble are planning a sneak attack?" Tomás asked.

"Nope. Their parents would never let them ride their bikes here in the dark—at least I hope not," reasoned Luke.

As the boys started dozing off, Tomás heard what sounded like a gi-normous rumble. "Wha-what was that?" he stuttered.

"Buuurrrppp!"

"There it is again!"

"Aw, that's just Burpie," chuckled Luke. "He ate too much pizza. He's not named *Burpie* for nothin'."

"That's a fact!" Harris added, as they all rolled with laughter.

Soon they were sound asleep. Luke began to dream a royal dream where warriors were courageous, knights were knightly, and castles were majestic.

Chapter Two – The Knightly Dream

"Hear ye! Hear ye, you sleepy three! You're going to the Castle of Calvary!" announced Constant, the King's royal helper. He was called Constant because he constantly forgot things and constantly spoke in rhyme. "You are invited to come with me. Warrior camp is where you'll see the kind of warrior God wants you to be

Luke, Harris, and Tomás jumped up and out of their sleeping bags. Burpie was immediately at their side. The boys couldn't believe their eyes!

Constant came to invite the boys to Warrior Prince Academy. They were going to learn how to become warrior princes for the King of kings.

Constant spotted Double and Trouble behind a larger-than-life sycamore tree and ordered, "You two behind that big old tree, you too must come and join these three. Hurry, hurry, or we'll be late. The camp begins. This is the date! The horses are waiting right outside. There's one for each of you to ride."

"I've never ridden a horse," Luke confessed, "and I don't plan to until pigs fly or horses talk!"

"Then hop on!" said a friendly voice.

"Who...who said that?" stuttered Luke.

"I did," answered a chocolate-colored, talking horse. "I'm Keydon, a horse in the King's royal army."

Luke nervously got on Keydon's back. The other boys did the same with horses of their own.

"Did you say the King has an army?" Tomás asked Keydon.

"I sure did."

"Cool! How do you join?" Double asked.

"You become a member of the King's army the moment you become a part of God's royal family," Keydon explained. "This makes you a warrior for Jesus!"

"Hear ye! Hear ye! Listen to me! You are at the Warrior Prince Academy!" Constant declared.

Trumpets blew as the boys entered the campsite. Huge tents were set up in front of the castle. The boys were amazed. A real knight stepped out to greet them, but this was no ordinary knight. It was Sir Britmore, one of the King's mighty men. He looked and sounded a lot like Coach Britmore. Could it really be him?

"Welcome boys!" said Sir Britmore. "Your journey has just begun. We have much to learn about what it means to be a warrior for the King of kings. And we don't have much time. It has been reported that Drakon, the snake, is sneaking around. Be alert! He'll stop at nothing to keep you from becoming a warrior prince!"

"Ha! Trouble and I aren't afraid of a little ol' snake!" Double taunted.

"Not so fast," warned Sir Britmore. "This snake may seem harmless, but he is cunning and a master of tricks and traps."

"If you aren't careful, you'll believe his lies and fall into the snares he's prepared for you. First things first. We must make sure you know what a warrior prince is."

"That's easy!" interrupted Double. "A warrior prince is rough and tough and likes to fight—like me!"

"That's what I thought until I met the King," said Sir Britmore. "He taught me that a warrior prince is a son of the King of kings. His purpose is to obey and serve the King. He never goes into battle without the King's command or protection."

"Yeah, right," whispered Double.

When they had gathered around the roaring campfire, Sir Britmore told them that the first step to becoming a warrior prince is to believe that Jesus died on the cross for their sins in order that they may be forgiven. By humbling themselves to accept Jesus' love and forgiveness and by placing their complete trust and their lives in God's hands, they will become victorious warriors just like the true Bible hero—a brave and simple shepherd boy named David.

"As in King David?" asked Luke.

"That's right, Luke. Before David was king, he tended sheep. One day, David's father asked him to go and check on his big brothers who were in the Israelite army. As David reached their camp, he heard the army shouting their battle cry."

"Howwwwwwllll!" barked Burpie, wagging his tail.

"I doubt their battle cry sounded quite like that," laughed the knight, and then he continued. "Instead of running *away* to safety, David ran *toward* the battlefield and lined up with the Israelite soldiers to face their enemy, the Philistines.

"As the armies prepared for battle, a Philistine giant named Goliath stepped forward, shouting and threatening the army of Israel. He stood taller than nine feet high, and he wore armor that weighed more than a hundred pounds. He roared when he spoke. Believing no one was brave enough to fight him, Goliath made fun of the Israelites and God."

"Sure," Trouble agreed. "How tall did you say he was?"

"Taller than you and Double put together," answered Sir Britmore. "David was surprised that the Israelite army was afraid of Goliath. They had God on their side, after all! So, David chose to fight the giant himself."

"I hope he wore heavy-duty armor!" said Tomás.

"No, he didn't wear any armor at all. David faced Goliath with only five smooth stones and his sling. When he met the giant, David said, 'You come against me with sword and spear and javelin, but I come against you in the name of the LORD Almighty!'"

"Excuse me, sir, but technically there's no way a boy could beat a giant," Harris calculated.

"Humanly speaking, that's true," Sir Britmore agreed, "but nothing is impossible with God, and David knew this. He ran toward Goliath shouting, 'I come against you in the name of the LORD!' Then he pulled back his sling and released a stone. It hit Goliath on his forehead. With a loud thump, Goliath fell dead. What was impossible for man, was possible with God. It was God's strength that helped David defeat Goliath. So remember, when you face your enemy, stand strong in the Lord."

"Cool!" said Double. "Do we get slingshot lessons?"

"I'm afraid not," answered Sir Britmore. "We'll continue tomorrow. Now, off to bed, all of you. You will sleep in the warrior-in-training tent tonight."

Chapter Four – The Snake Hunt

Luke thought about being a warrior as he tried to sleep, but noises outside kept him awake. He looked out of the tent and saw Double and Trouble running into the woods with something that looked like a snake right behind them!

"Come on, Burpie," Luke said, grabbing a flashlight. "We have to get to Double and Trouble before Drakon does!"

Luke and Burpie ran toward the woods. They soon found themselves in a thicket of tall trees, and out of the corner of his eye, Luke saw something move. He whispered, "I think they went this way."

"Boo!" shouted Double and Trouble, jumping out from behind a tree.

"Gotcha good!" laughed Double, pushing Luke toward Trouble.

"Yeah!" agreed Trouble, pushing Luke back toward Double. "How come you're following us?"

"To warn you about Drakon," said Luke. "I saw him."

"Good!" replied Double. "We're on a snake hunt to prove we're not afraid of him!"

"I don't think that's a good idea," Luke said. "Let's just go back to the camp before he finds us."

"Why? Are you scared?" asked Double.

"Some brave warrior you are!" teased Trouble, as he and Double ran off in search of Drakon.

Luke and Burpie were alone. Luke just wanted to go back to camp and forget this happened. As he turned to leave, he heard a slithery voice—a voice that made the hairs on the back of his neck stand up.

"What'sss your hurry?" the voice hissed from a tree.

"Dra-Drakon, is that you?" sputtered Luke, peering into the tree as Burpie ran to the castle for help.

"Yesss, it'sss me. Who elssse were you expecting?" questioned Drakon.

Luke's heart was racing, but he remembered what Sir Britmore said. *When you face your enemy, stand strong in the Lord.* Luke quickly prayed, "Jesus, please help me to be brave in Your strength!"

"Go away Drakon!" Luke yelled. "Leave me alone!"

"Isss that anyway to greet a friend?" asked Drakon.

"You're not my friend!" said Luke. "You like to trick people."

"You're jussst afraid," teased Drakon. "Don't you want to be a brave and powerful warrior prince?"

"How do you know that?" Luke asked.

"I know lotsss of thingsss—like how you're ssscared of Double and Trouble," Drakon said. "A real warrior wouldn't be afraid. You shouldn't either."

Part of what Drakon said was true. Luke was afraid of the twins, but he didn't know what to do about it.

"I've got an idea," said Drakon. "Get even with them. Jussst tell them you found me. When they come running, jump out and punch them in the nossse. They'll neve expect that—sssuch sssneaky fun!"

"A warrior prince of the King of the kings would never treat his teammates that ay," growled Luke.

"Come on! It'll be our sssecret," encouraged Drakon. "Besssidesss, they dessserve it

Luke knew they deserved it, but voices interrupted Luke's thoughts.

"Help! Help!"

It was Double and Trouble. Luke had to find them, so he took off running. Drakon lithered close behind.

"Double! Trouble!" yelled Luke. "Where are you?"

"Down here!" they shouted. "We fell into a pit!"

"You don't really want to help them—do you?" whispered Drakon. "Jussst think of ll the timesss they weren't nice to you, behavior unbecoming of princely warriorsss."

Luke didn't fall for it. "I'm doing the right thing," Luke said, reaching for Double's hand.

"Can I be of any asssissstance?" asked Drakon, peering at Double and Trouble.

Double loosened his grip on Luke's hand at the sound of Drakon's voice.

"Don't let go!" Luke shouted, but it was too late. Double dropped back into the pit.

"If Drakon's up there, we're staying down here!" Double said fearfully.

"Your friendsss act more like ssscardey catsss than noble warriorsss," laughed Drakon.

"Hey! Don't make fun of my teammates!" Luke said, defending the twins.

"You tell him buddy!" Double and Trouble called out to Luke.

"Of courssse," agreed Drakon, "I've forgotten my mannersss. Let me make it up to you. I'll make you all brave warriorsss. All you have to do isss obey me."

"No way!" said Luke, courageously looking Drakon in the eye. "King Jesus is the only leader we will obey. It is in Jesus' name that I stand strong!"

At the mention of Jesus' name, Drakon quickly ducked and slithered away. Luke reached back down and helped Double and Trouble out of the pit.

"Look at him go!" laughed Double.

"I didn't know a snake could wiggle that fast!" added Trouble.

"He may return," said Luke. "Let's get back to camp."

Trumpets blared upon their return. The entire camp had been searching for them. First, they saw Burpie leading the way. Then, they saw Sir Britmore ride into view. Harris, Tomás, and the entire royal army followed closely behind. Double shouted, "You missed it! Luke just battled Drakon and won!"

"Well done, Luke!" Sir Britmore proudly said beaming.

"All I did was pray. God did the rest! With His strength, I had the courage to stand up to Drakon," said Luke.

"Spoken like a true warrior prince!" declared Sir Britmore, as Burpie jumped up and licked Luke as if to say, "Job well done!"

Sluuurp!

Luke woke from his dream to find Burpie licking his face. He sat straight up in his sleeping bag and said, "I really *can* be a noble and brave warrior prince with God's help!"

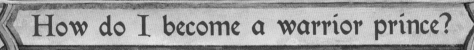

How do I become a warrior prince?

It's easy to say and do things to make the people you love happy. Becoming a son of the King is more than that! You must truly love Jesus with all of your heart, and because of that, you must really want to connect with Him in a genuine relationship. That's when God becomes your Father in heaven and you know that you are a son of the King!

You must believe that Jesus died on the cross for your sins and that He was raised again three days later. Sins are the bad things we do. They are things like lying, disobeying, and being selfish.

For God so loved the world that he gave his one and only Son, that whoever believes in him shall not perish but have eternal life.—John 3:16

Then pray and tell Jesus that you want Him to be Lord of your life because you love Him and believe He died for you.

If you confess with your mouth, "Jesus is Lord," and believe in your heart that God raised him from the dead, you will be saved.—Romans 10:9

The moment you believe in Jesus, He comes to live in your heart as Lord and Savior, and you become a real prince, a son of the King of kings. You can be a warrior prince by obeying and trusting only in God and standing bravely in His name.

"I will be a Father to you, and you will be my sons and daughters," says the Lord Almighty.—2 Corinthians 6:18

You will also live happily-ever-after in eternity with Jesus one day.

For the wages of sin is death, but the gift of God is eternal life in Christ Jesus our Lord.—Romans 6:23

A Royal Prince Prayer

Dear Jesus,

I know that I have sin in my life. I know I can't get rid of my sin by doing good things. I need You to take it away. I believe You died on the cross for me and that You rose again. I want You to be Lord of my life. I will obey and trust only You. Help me to stand bravely in Your name. Thank You, Jesus, for coming to live in my heart. I am now a warrior prince!

Hear ye! Hear ye!

Let it be known throughout the land,

Warrior Prince_____
is now part of God's royal plan!

For he believed and now Jesus lives in his heart,
where He will live forever and never depart.
He also believes Jesus died on the cross for his sins,
and three days later, He rose again.

The date he believed,

_____,

whereupon the angels did sing,
was the day they celebrated his becoming a
warrior prince of the King of kings!